The Adventures of Drew and Ellie

The Magical Dress

By Charles Noland

Illustrated by Sherri Baker

TMD

Rochester, NY

Second Edition
© 2006 by Charles Noland. All rights reserved.

First published 2003

Published by TMD Enterprises, Rochester, NY

Library of Congress Control Number: 2006908233
ISBN 13: 978-0-9789297-0-1
ISBN 10:   0-9789297-0-5 (previously ISBN 1-4140-3500-4)

This book is printed on acid free paper.

Printed in the United States of America

This book is dedicated to Chris and Katie. Your spirit and sense of adventure provided me with the inspiration for the characters in this book. You both are truly wonderful gifts from God.

Table of Contents

❧ 1 ❧

Saturday Morning Surprise

Andrew was playing with his action hero toys on the floor in the living room while his sister Ellen watched a movie. It was a Saturday morning in the early fall, and it was right after breakfast.

Occasionally, they would both glance toward the window watching the weather outside. They were hoping it wouldn't rain so that they could go to the playground later in the day. They loved going to the playground—it was where all their friends were, and they could play all kinds of adventurous games with them.

Together, they lived with their mother in a very nice apartment in a very nice neighborhood. As brother and sister, they always did everything together, and most people referred to them as Drew and Ellie—unless of course, you were mad at them, and then it was Andrew and Ellen.

Suddenly, Drew and Ellie's mom came into the room. "I have a surprise for the two of you," she said.

Drew and Ellie swung around from where they were sitting to face their mom. She was holding a very large shopping bag.

She sat down on the couch and asked, "Do you remember my friend Mrs. Williams?"

They both nodded.

"Well, the other day she told me she had some clothes to give me that her kids had outgrown, and here they are."

"Cool!" said Drew. "Let's see them."

So, their mom began to unpack the clothes from the bag. Since Mrs. Williams had two boys and only one girl, most of the clothes were for Drew. However, there were a few pairs of pants and a couple of dresses for Ellie.

As she got to the bottom of the bag, she seemed surprised to find another bag. She pulled it out, and in it was a beautiful, white dress with a sparkly look to it. Ellie's eyes lit up.

"*Momma,* I want to try that dress on. Can I?"

Ellie's mom looked the dress over and said, "This looks almost brand new. I wonder how this got in here?"

Ellie persisted. "Can I try that dress on now, *please?*"

"Okay," said Ellie's mom. "Come over here, and let's see how it looks."

Ellie raced over to the couch and immediately started putting the dress on

"Hold on a minute," her mom said. "Let's get these other clothes off first."

After Ellie got the dress on, she went upstairs to her bedroom to find a pair of white stockings from her dresser. Then she went into the closet to find her black shoes to complete the outfit. She waltzed back downstairs and into the living room.

"Wow, don't you look fashionable!" exclaimed her mother.

Ellie loved the dress and the white, sparkly fabric. She was only four, but already she loved getting dressed up with fancy clothes. She danced around the room a few times, twirling and pretending she was at a beautiful ball.

As she was dancing, the phone rang, and their mom got up and left the room. Drew, who was seven and less interested in dressing up, watched her twirl a few more times and then went back to playing with his action hero toys.

When Ellie grew bored with twirling, she decided that she was going to have a party with some of her dolls, so she went upstairs to her bedroom to find all of her guests.

❧ 2 ❧

A Magical Discovery

While Ellie was putting together her guests for her party, she discovered that she was missing her favorite one, Sally. She looked all over her room and even went down into Drew's room, but she could not find her. Walking back into her bedroom, she wondered where Sally could be. As she stood there, she looked down at the beautiful, white, sparkly fabric of her new dress. Drawn to it, she began to stroke it with her hand. It was so pretty. She closed her eyes, wishing she could remember where Sally was, when suddenly there was a bright, sparkly light.

Ellie opened her eyes and looked up. As the light faded, there, right in front of her, was Sally, her favorite doll.

Ellie looked confused. She ran downstairs to get her mom, but her mom was on the phone talking to Grandma. She ran into the living room to talk to Drew, but he was too busy playing with his action hero toys. Giving up, she went back upstairs to her dolls to finish having her party.

Although she had assembled everyone and gotten them all seated, Ellie didn't really feel like playing anymore. She was still thinking about what had happened earlier with Sally. Curious about the dress, Ellie decided to try something new.

She sat down next to her dolls and started stroking the dress again, closing her eyes. This time, however, she wished for some of her favorite string cheese. Just as before, there was a bright, sparkly light, and as she opened her eyes and the light faded, there on the floor was a package of her favorite string cheese.

This is pretty neat, she thought, as she opened it and peeled off a piece.

She continued playing, enjoying her snack, when Drew walked into the room.

"Hey Ellie, let's play a game," he said.

"What kind of a game?" Ellie responded.

"One of our adventure games. You know, where we imagine going places like the safari we went on," said Drew.

"Before we play," Ellie started, "I have to tell you about this dress – I think it is *magical*."

Drew wasn't completely listening—he was too busy trying to move the dolls so he could sit down and tell Ellie about where they could go on their adventure.

Ellie motioned for Drew to pay attention. "Watch this," she said.

Ellie closed her eyes and started stroking her dress while she wished for Drew's action hero toys from downstairs. Again, there a bright, sparkly light—even Drew saw it, too. As the light faded, there on the floor right next to Drew were his action hero toys.

"COOL!" exclaimed Drew. "How did you do that?"

Ellie explained that the dress was somehow magical. "All I have to do is rub my hand on the dress while I wish for something, and then there is a bright light. When the light goes away, whatever I wished for just magically appears."

As Drew leaned forward to touch the dress, there was a flash of lightning outside, followed by a big clap of thunder, and then it began to pour. They both got up and went over to the window. Looking out, they realized that they would not be going to the playground today.

"Darn!" Drew said sadly. "I was hoping we could have gone out today. I don't want to spend another weekend indoors. Why can't it be nice out like it was in the summer when we were camping back at the lake?"

"Yeah," said Ellie. "Do you remember how much fun we had at the beach, and how we played all day in the water?"

"That was awesome!" Drew replied. "Now *that* would be a fun place to go on our adventure!"

Ellie smiled and looked at Drew. "Wait a minute I have an idea."

❧ 3 ❧

Back to the Beach

"I think we might be able to go back to the beach," Ellie said.

"How?" asked Drew.

"What if we could wish our way there using this magical dress, the same way I wished for your action hero toys from downstairs?" replied Ellie.

"Well, I think that would be cool, but do you think we could really do it?"

"We could try it, but first," Ellie said, sitting back down, "I think we would both have to wish for the same thing at the same time, together."

"All right," said Drew. "Let's try."

So the two of them practiced exactly what they would wish for. As they got comfortable on the floor next to each other, Ellie turned to her brother.

"When I count to three, we both start wishing that we were back at the beach, just like we practiced, okay?"

Drew nodded.

Ellie took Drew's hand and started stroking the dress with her other hand. Closing her eyes, she said, "One, two, three!"

Both Drew and Ellie started wishing they were back at the beach. Suddenly, there was a very bright, sparkly light before them. As they opened their eyes and the light faded, they found themselves sitting on the grass right smack in front of the beach. They both screamed with delight and got up and ran toward the water. As they got closer, they stopped long enough to take off their shoes, socks, and stockings before wading in. They both knew about water safety, so they didn't go in very far.

It was a beautiful, hot, sunny day and Drew said, "This is exactly like when we were here this summer!"

Ellie agreed as she started splashing around in the warm water.

Before long, they were both soaked to the bone and their clothes were plastered against them as if they had been painted on.

Ellie turned to Drew and said, "Let's go over to a picnic table, and I will wish us some ice cream."

"Great idea!" yelled Drew.

They both raced from the water and ran to one of the picnic tables shaded by a row of big pine trees.

When they got there, Ellie sat down on the seat. Closing her eyes, she started stroking her dress. She wished for two big dishes of their favorite ice cream with two spoons, but after a minute had passed, nothing happened. There was no bright, sparkly light, and when she opened her eyes, she saw only a blank table. Squirming around in the puddle of water on the seat, she closed her eyes again.

Stroking the dress, she began wishing for the ice cream, but still nothing happened.

Looking at his sister, Drew asked, "What's wrong?"

"I don't know," she quickly replied. She tried it again and again, and all with the same results—nothing.

"Drew, it's not working!" Ellie said, frustrated.

"Now just slow down for a minute, Ellie, and concentrate like before." Drew tried to sound comforting.

So Ellie tried one more time, only this time she really concentrated hard. Unfortunately, it still didn't work. There was no bright, sparkly light and definitely no ice cream.

❧ 4 ❧

It's Looking Hopeless

"Maybe we should try and find someone to help us so we can get back home," Drew suggested. "We could go over to one of the campground buildings and look."

Ellie agreed, and the two of them started walking over to one of the first little buildings following a narrow stone path.

"Ow!" cried Ellie. "These stones are hurting my feet."

"Walk over here," said Drew, as he grabbed his sister and pulled her off the path. "On the grass along the edge." She followed along behind him.

As they walked up to the first building, they both noticed a padlock on the door.

"It looks like it is all locked up," observed Ellie.

"Yeah it does, but maybe I can look through the window and see if there is someone staying here," said Drew.

Unfortunately, the windowsill was just a little too tall for him, so he really couldn't get a good look inside. He even tried jumping up to get a look, but it didn't help.

Ellie went over and knocked on the door. No one answered.

Giving up, Drew said, "Let's try another building."

They walked further along the path to the next little building and were met with pretty much the same results—a locked door and nobody around.

Ellie looked at Drew and said, "Why don't we try one of the big buildings over there?" She pointed across the big, grassy field.

"Okay," Drew said, and they walked across the grassy field to the biggest building first.

"This is where I got the bandage for my knee when I fell down hiking," Ellie said.

Drew nodded. "I remember that."

They walked all around the building, knocking on all three of the doors they found. Still there was no answer, but then Drew spotted a sign in one of the windows. He ran over to it and read it out loud for Ellie to hear.

"Closed for the season," he said sadly. "I guess that's why there's no one around."

They slowly headed back across the grassy field, this time to another picnic table that was in the sun.

Realizing that they were all alone, Ellie started to cry. "I wish we were back home with Mom right now," she whimpered.

Drew walked over to his sister and put his arm around her. "Don't cry, Ellie. You know what Mom would say if she were here right now don't you?"

She looked up at Drew with tears in her eyes and replied, "She would tell us to use our problem-solving skills."

"Right," said Drew confidently. "So, let's figure this out together."

"Okay," Ellie said, wiping away the tears that had run down her cheek.

❧ 5 ❧

Figuring it Out

When they reached the picnic table, Ellie sat down and began to think.

Drew turned to Ellie and asked, "Okay, now how were you able to make the dress work before?"

Ellie shrugged. "All I had to do was stroke the side of my dress and wish for what I wanted."

Drew paced back and forth in front of Ellie, thinking of his next question. "Did you have your eyes open or closed when you did it?"

Ellie thought for a moment and then said, "Closed at first, then I remember opening them when I saw the sparkly light."

Drew walked over to Ellie. "Well, let's try that right now, just the way you said."

So, Ellie sat straight up, closed her eyes, and started stroking the dress, again wishing for some ice cream. Nothing happened.

Drew then suggested that she try it standing up.

So, Ellie got up, stood next to the table, and tried it again. Nothing happened.

Suddenly, Drew exclaimed, "Wait a minute! Weren't you sitting down on the floor when you did it before?"

Ellie nodded as she remembered, then moved away from the table and sat on the ground. She closed her eyes and started stroking the dress again while she wished for the ice cream. But, try and try as she might, it still didn't work.

Looking very frustrated, Ellie got up and walked back to the picnic table. Just as she was about to sit down, Drew noticed something.

"Hey Ellie, your dress is getting kind of dirty.
You have sand all over the back of it."

Ellie looked at Drew and her eyes got bigger. "Maybe the dress doesn't work if it is dirty and not sparkly."

Drew thought Ellie could be right, so they both walked back down to the beach to the edge of the water. Together, they carefully rinsed the sand and the dirt off the dress the best they could.

As they were doing that, Drew suddenly jumped up and looked at his sister, calling out, "Ellie, I think I figured it out! When you were using the dress before, and it worked, the dress was dry and not wet!"

A huge smile appeared on Ellie's face. "You're right! So all we have to do is dry out the dress and try it again."

With that, they both walked out of the water and made their way across the grassy field back to one of the picnic tables in the sun.

❧ 6 ❧

Drying Out

On the way to the picnic table, Drew turned to Ellie and said, "I have another idea. What if you were to stand on top of the table and maybe let the wind dry your dress?"

"Okay, let's try it," Ellie replied.

When they got to the table, Drew helped his sister climb up on top of it. She proceeded to walk back and forth, twirling around as if she were dancing. There wasn't any wind though, and there was barely even a breeze.

After a few minutes, she looked down at her brother and said, "I don't think it is really working too well."

So, he helped her down, and she stood next to the table thinking.

"Wait a minute," said Ellie. "Why don't we run down to the beach and then back up to the building and see if that will help dry out the dress?"

"Sure," said Drew.

So, they both ran down to the beach and then back up to the building and then down to the beach again.

Ellie stopped to catch her breath. "I'm getting tired," she said, panting.

Drew touched her dress and then looked at her, smiling. "I think it is working; it feels drier to me."

"How about we walk for a while?" suggested Ellie.

They walked back up to the building and then down to the beach a couple more times until Ellie finally stopped Drew and said, "I am so tired. I want to go lie down and rest now."

Drew walked with her over to a grassy area in the shade. He took off his shirt and told her to lie down on it so that she would not get her dress any dirtier. Ellie lay down and curled up so she could stay on the shirt. Within minutes, she was fast asleep.

Drew paced back and forth for a while and then decided to sit down next to his sister so he could watch over her. As he sat down and got comfortable, he realized that he was also pretty tired, and before long, he was fast asleep beside her.

After a few hours, a crow flying overhead suddenly called out and startled Ellie awake. It took her a minute to figure out where she was, and then she woke Drew up.

As Drew opened his eyes, he looked up and then out across the lake and saw that the sun was starting to go down.

Turning to his sister, he said, "It's getting late, and we need to get home."

Ellie felt her dress. It was completely dry except for a very small area in the back where she had been lying on Drew's shirt.

"Come on!" she exclaimed. "My dress is dry. Let's go try it."

❧ 7 ❧

Going Home

Ellie raced back over to the picnic table that was in the sun. She stopped as she approached it and, closing her eyes, started stroking her dress. Suddenly, there was the bright, sparkly light, but this time it was different. And when she opened her eyes, she found just one small dish of ice cream.

"It works again!" yelled Drew, coming up behind her.

"No, something is still wrong," said Ellie. "I wished for *two* large dishes of ice cream, not one small one."

"Oh," Drew said, perplexed. "Well, maybe it's not working right because the dress is still wet somewhere."

Ellie showed him the spot where the dress was still damp. Drew felt it and said, "Listen, it's going to be dark pretty soon, and we really need to get home. I don't think we can wait much longer. We'll have to try it."

Ellie protested. "I'm hungry, and we haven't eaten anything all day. Can't we just eat this ice cream?"

Drew looked at his sister and smiled. "All right, let's eat it quick," he said.

So, they both shared the dish of ice cream, which tasted pretty good after such a hot and tiring day.

Afterward, they raced down to the beach area to put their stockings, socks, and shoes back on.

Walking back up to the table, Ellie said, "We should practice again what we are going to wish for, and maybe we should even say it out loud this time."

Drew looked at his sister and said, "Good idea."

They both practiced for a few minutes exactly what they were going to say. Next, they settled down on the grass and got comfortable.

"Remember now, on the count of three," said Ellie, crossing her legs.

Just then, Ellie looked at Drew with concern and said, "Wait a minute I only got one dish of ice cream, remember? What if only one of us can go back?"

"We can't think that way, Ellie. We have to concentrate real hard. Your dress is almost completely dry; it will work!" replied Drew, taking hold of his sister's hand. He closed his eyes and said, "Ready?"

Ellie closed her eyes and squeezed her brother's hand, then started stroking the side of her dress. "ONE, TWO, THREE!" she shouted.

In unison, they both yelled out, "We wish we were back home in Ellie's room watching it rain outside like this morning!"

Suddenly, there was a very bright, sparkly light, and as they opened their eyes and the light faded, they found themselves sitting in Ellie's bedroom facing the window as the rain came down.

❦ 8 ❧

Home – The Best Place to Be

"IT WORKED!" they yelled gleefully.

"What worked?" asked their mom.

They both turned around and saw their mom standing in the doorway of Ellie's bedroom.

"MOM!" they said excitedly. And with that, they both got up and ran over to her, giving her big hugs.

"WOW!" she said, surprised by all the excitement and affection. "This is quite a greeting. So, what were the two of you doing?"

"Ellie and I went on another adventure," Drew replied.

"Yeah, and we're just glad to be back here with you," chimed Ellie.

"Well, I don't know where you went this time, but I'm glad to have you back here, too," she said, returning their hugs.

Pulling away, she asked them, "Would you like to go downstairs to the kitchen and have a snack of juice and string cheese?"

"Yeah!" they both said together.

Turning to Ellie, she said, "But first, we need to get this nice dress off of you so you don't get it dirty."

Drew started gathering up his action hero toys as she helped Ellie take the dress off.

"That's funny," she said, surprised, "I hadn't noticed this small grass stain before when you put the dress on. I guess it wasn't new after all."

Drew looked back at his sister, who was smiling, and winked at her.

"All right then," said their mom, pulling a sweatshirt on over Ellie's head. "Why don't you both put away your toys and dolls, and I will go down to the kitchen and get your snack ready. And while I'm at it, I'd better see if I can get the grass stain out of this dress, too."

"Okay," they replied.

As Ellie finished putting away her last doll, she walked over to her big brother and hugged him.

"Thanks for helping me on our adventure," she said gratefully.

Drew hugged her back and replied, "I think we both helped each other, and remember, we figured it out together."

As it thundered again, they both glanced back at the window and saw the rain coming down outside. Then taking each other's hand, they skipped through the bedroom door and down to the kitchen where there was a cup of juice and some string cheese waiting for each of them.

The End.

Join Drew and Ellie in their next adventure with the Magical Dress as they go to the Mountains of New Hampshire in...

The Daring Rescue

Ellie leaned over the edge of the path, looking down the slope of a long embankment to the trail below. "There it is!" She exclaimed.

"Where?" asked Drew. "I don't see it."

"It's on the rock down there by the pine tree," she said, pointing to the orange dot that marked the trail they were supposed to be on.

"I still don't see it," Drew said, frustrated.

As Ellie turned to her brother to find out where he was looking, her left foot slipped on the dry pine needles and leaves that were all over the ground. Suddenly, she lost her balance, fell backwards onto her backpack, and started sliding down the steep hill.

"Drew! Drew!" she screamed. "Help me!"

Drew lunged for his sister's hand but it was too late. He watched in amazement as she slid down the steep embankment.

Halfway down, the straps from her backpack came off her shoulders and one of them caught the branch of a fallen tree. She stopped for a brief moment, but then the backpack slipped off, and she continued to slide the rest of the way down the hill.

When she finally reached the bottom, she slowly stood up. She could hear Drew yelling to her from the top.

"Ellie! Are you all right?"

"Yes, I guess so," she replied, a bit shaken. Then she thought it over. "Actually, it was kind of fun. It was a little like sledding. Only not as cold."

"Great," he replied with a heavy sigh. "Now what are we going to do?"

Drew looked down the embankment at his sister, who was a good fifty feet away, and then at the backpack that was still stuck on the tree branch. In the backpack was the magical dress. And without it, they were never going to get back home.

Do you want to know more about Drew and Ellie?
Visit their web site at

www.drewandellie.com

Coloring pages, reader's comments and more!

About the author: *The Magical Dress* is Charles Noland's first book for children. Inspired by two youngsters who embody a playful spirit and sense of adventure, Noland created the characters of Drew and Ellie to serve as role models for positive sibling relations. In addition to wanting to entertain and delight young readers, he believes in creating stories that teach good values and important life lessons.

Noland is a business professional with experience in management and sales, as well as an accomplished speaker, engaging storyteller and avid reader. A native and resident of Rochester, N.Y., he is currently working on the next adventure for Drew, Ellie and the Magical Dress.

About the illustrator: Sherri Baker always dreamed of illustrating children's books – creating the engaging pictures for *The Magical Dress* helped make that dream a reality. Ever since she was a child herself, Baker has had a passion for both art and literature, which provides her with a keen understanding of the images and stories that engage children the most. She enjoys creating illustrations for young, imaginative minds, especially the pen and ink drawings she created for the first book in this series.

A native of Upstate New York, Baker studied studio art at Nazareth College, concentrating in illustration and computer graphics. She continues to work in commercial advertising as an illustrator and designer. She currently lives in Rochester, NY.